Professor Odd #4

Other Heliopause Productions:

THE ADVENTURES OF BOURAGNER FELPZ
Volume I: A Study of Magic

APSIS FICTION
The Semi-Annual Anthology of Goldeen Ogawa

PROFESSOR ODD
#1 The False Student
#2 The Slowly Dying Planet
#3 The Promethean Predicament

heliopauseweb.com

PROFESSOR ODD
THE ELDER MACHINE

Professor Odd #4

by
GOLDEEN OGAWA

a Heliopause Production

Prologue

A TALL THIN FIGURE in a tattered overcoat walked forlornly along the river. In the yellow light from the streetlamps its shadow was cast deep and black into the water.

Movement in the river; the swish and swirl of disturbed water, and the figure paused. Stopped. Turned and looked. It crouched down by the water's edge and reached a hand out across the surface.

With a muffled cry and a splash the figure disappeared suddenly into the river, casting water up onto the bricks of the path. Somewhere in the night a dog barked.

Then quiet. The river ran smooth once more.

Part One

THE FEELING CREPT, like tendrils of unpleasant slime, through his mind. The feeling of *wrongness*, that the natural order of things was being violated, and he paused in his writing and stared out at the peaceful lawn, with its scattered herds of brightly colored tourists milling about, until the feeling passed.

The Journal of Dr Alister Bane
Professor of Archeology, GTC, Oxford
June 11th, 20–, 10:18 AM
front steps of the Museum of Natural History

I am having migraines again. At least, that is what I think they are. They come on strong and fast, give me a few moments of blinding pain, and then leave just as quickly. They seem to be triggered at random, sometimes striking me while at table, sometimes while walking to breakfast. On occasion I think it is something I have seen that triggers them—something in the corner of my vision that contradicts what should be. I think there is information in these blinding flashes, but such information as would be anathema for my brain to comprehend.

They do not seem to do me any tangible harm, so I have begun keeping this journal as a way of tracking them, their frequency, and the situations surrounding their occurrence. In this way I hope to collate some useful information, and to ascertain whether they are increasing.

The most recent case manifested in the last hour while I was walking back from the Pitt Rivers. Doing so necessitates passing through the main hall of the MNH, past the dinosaur skeletons and the stuffed animals. The MNH has a seemingly endless supply of preserved ponies, big cats, and birds of all sizes propped up on wires behind glass, and as I passed through, my eye was drawn to the shelf of preserved sea fauna, strung up in preservative fluid. There I had the most disconcerting feeling of seeing something wrong: one of the specimens—some kind of squid—had been dyed a bright green by an accident of chemicals, and its eyes appeared much brighter and alive. Some precocious child, rocketing through the aisle, clipped the case and sent the fluid sloshing, causing the many puckered arms and tentacles to wave lazily at me, as if in greeting.

It was then I began to feel the ache in my sinuses, and I managed to escape from that wretched place and collapse on the steps before the whiteness overcame my vision.

Having just recovered I determined to begin setting down an account of these incidents, in the hope that some rhyme or reason may become apparent. And this I have just done.

Doctor Alister Bane put his pen away and closed the little book. He rose from the steps of the Museum of Natural History— slowly, because he still felt slightly ill—and walked purposefully across the lawn. The comforting sounds of Oxford in late spring, the rumble of traffic and the softer, yet no less pervasive, hum of human voices, swelled around him and soothed his frazzled nerves.

The walk from Pitt Rivers to his college was not a strenuous one, but Alister liked the way his moving legs stirred the thoughts in his mind and let them settle into new shapes. Walks, he had decided when still an undergraduate, were the best thing for thinking. Better than rowing, which you had to prepare for, and better far than any kind of organized sport, where your teammates would not understand why you had to sit down in the middle of a play to jot down notes. Walking also helped shake the remaining twinges from his mind, and he was feeling quite himself again as he crossed Banbury Road and cut between St Giles and its graveyard.

It being a pleasant, sunny day, the graveyard was unusually cheerful and noisy; a little island of shade and trees and grass set between two busy streets, it was temporarily home to a number of lunching couples, a few students with laptops, and a girl in a red coat playing fetch with a large golden dog.

This dog, much to Alister's annoyance, took an immediate interest in him and came tearing across the grass, dodging between gravestones, skidding to a stop at his feet. For one horrible second he thought it would tackle him, but it only nosed at his hand and, even as the little girl came running, shouting "Bad dog!" in her shrill young voice, it pressed something small and wet and a little pulpy into his hand.

Then it was off, running away from its mistress, barking and flapping its feathered tail excitedly.

Alister stood holding the clammy damp blob in his hand, struck dumb. Then, as if moving under the directions of a mind other than his own, he calmly unfolded the tacky paper. There, in blobby blue ballpoint pen, were scratched the words:

Don't be afraid to look in the cracks.

—Odd

Coming back to himself Alister dropped the paper and began walking briskly down Woodstock Road, trying to shake the feeling that he had seen that handwriting before somewhere. Sometime a long time ago. When he was a student? But it hadn't been in Oxford, that was for certain, and Alister had done his entire tenure at Green Templeton. Where then?

A dull ache in his jaw, quickly spreading to his sinuses, and Alister just had the willpower to throw himself against the nearest wall before the whiteness flashed behind his eyes.

The Journal of Dr Alister Bane
Professor of Archeology, GTC, Oxford
June 11th 20–, 12:02 PM
the Observatory, Green Templeton College, Oxford

I had not one, but two migraines—if they are indeed that—on my way back from the museum. In the first instance I saw some handwriting that triggered an obscure memory, and in trying to place it I suffered another attack. No sooner had I recovered than I looked across the road and saw one of our city's numerous street performers, apparently headed for the High. He appeared to be a blind juggler, for he wore thick dark glasses and walked with the long cane of those afflicted with that handicap. He carried a brace of clubs under his arm, and wore the most unlikely wig: bright yellow streaked with pink and teal. I only caught a passing glimpse of him, but the sight affected me dramatically. I had the strangest urge to run after him, a feeling that to lose him in the crowd of Oxford would be the worst of calamities. I was so upset that I barely noticed the warning signs, and the intense pain took me completely by surprise.

I stopped in at the Infirmary on my way back to GTC, and Dr Llewelyn was able to spare me a few minutes. From his initial examination there appears to be nothing wrong with me. He attributes the headaches to stress and has prescribed a mild sedative. I am dubious of its effectiveness, and I doubt I will take it: my current research demands so much energy I cannot afford to be sedated.

The Didcot Excavation was a young dig, the ink still drying on the permit, but it was already yielding rich results. What had begun as a lucky break for a farmer with a metal detector had quickly turned into the greatest opportunity of the century for any archeologist in Oxfordshire. A Roman treasure cache, priceless in itself, turned out to be only the beginning: below it was a bronze age burial, and below that stone age artifacts. Some intrepid researchers were arguing for digging further, that three discoveries from three different ages could not be a coincidence.

Alister was one of the most vocal proponents of continuing to dig down, so while he sorted through the wealth of artifacts brought back from the dig, he also drafted letters and appeals, trying to win over the more timid hearts.

While engaged in this altogether pleasurable task he was roused by a frantic tapping sound, as of fists hammering on glass. Alister jumped all over, and the sound resolved itself into the deep thumping of human hands on wood; someone was knocking at his door. A moment later it opened and his assistant tumbled into the room, shedding papers.

Alister stared. Margaret Barnes was usually defined by her neatness, her efficiency. Now she looked anything but neat; her brown hair was coming out of the tight bun in long strands and her normally starched and pressed shirt was rumpled and her sleeves rolled up to her elbows. She was carrying a stack of files, helplessly grabbing at the escaping sheets as they slipped from her arms.

"What bee has gotten in your bonnet, child?" Alister asked, catching a slim folder as it went flying.

"You didn't receive the bulletin, Professor?" Barnes returned, clutching the papers to her chest and looking stricken.

Alister gestured to the crowd of artifacts on his desk. "I have been otherwise occupied, I cannot check the bulletin every five minutes."

"It's Dr Cridget, Professor, he was brought up from the dig this morning—they say he's gone mad!"

Again Alister felt a cold feeling like slime dripping down his back, but this time there was no wavering of reality, it was simply a physical reaction to distressing news. Dr Cridget was an eminent researcher, and a friend—as far as Alister had friends.

"Where is he?"

"Still on site, as far as I know." Barnes held out a set of blue sheets with a shaking hand. "It says he's too unstable to move. But here's the dispatch for you. Dr Carly said she would call."

Snatching the sheets from the woman's unresisting hand, Alister dashed to the door and took the stairs two at a time as he hurtled out of the building. When he reached the street he groped in his pocket and brought out his cell phone—it *had* been on Silent this whole morning! And there was a message from Dr Carly—bless her, it was a text.

Cridget poorly. Need your advice. Meet at dig 30E.

The really impressive thing to do would be to hire a cab and have it drive him to the scene as fast as possible, but in Oxford on a Sunday afternoon Alister knew that would be only slightly faster than walking. Slower, if there had been an accident. So he jogged along the railing until he came to his bicycle, unlocked it, and mounted at a run, something he hadn't done since he was a boy. He nearly ran over a student as he pushed off into the road, but it hardly mattered. What mattered was that he was moving, and he was doing something.

From across the street, a large golden dog watched with interest.

The dig was halfway between Oxford proper and Didcot, located predominantly in a field which, up until a few months ago, had been home to a group of placid dairy cattle. Now the cattle were gone, and in their place a small city of white tents and awnings had sprung up. Cars, vans, and even a couple of lorries rolled over the uneven ground, leaving deep brown tracks in the grass within the designated traffic areas—which had been marked by yellow string stretched between orange posts.

One van pulled up outside a tent marked with a red cross, and Professor Bane tumbled out, still clutching his bicycle. He'd been passed by the shuttle crew outside of Oxford and given a lift, but he was still out of breath and very red and sweaty when he pushed aside the opening flaps of tent 30E and nearly walked straight into Dr Carly.

Dr Carly was a woman of mature years, her hair resolutely gray and her face as drooping as a bloodhound's. Today this impression was exaggerated by the overall drooping of her shoulders and her lab coat, which was pulled sideways and hanging off her arms.

"I heard—Cridget, is he—?" Alister couldn't bring himself to finish the question.

Dr Carly sighed heavily. "Oh, he's alive right enough. I hoped you might be able to get some sense out of him. Follow me. You worked 30E together, that so?"

"Aye," said Alister, following the doctor's slumped shoulders as she led the way deeper into the maze of white tent. "But 30E was never our prize dig; it was all broken bits and ends. I thought he'd be working 25B, or maybe C . . . "

"Well, this morning he must have found something. Or something found him. Put this on." She handed Alister a paper mask. "We're not sure what he's got. And for the love of Pete, don't upset him."

Dr Cridget had always been a nervous man. Maybe it went with the name; Alister thought if he had been called *Cridget* all his life he would be nervous as well. But his old quirks and tics were nothing compared to what Alister found in the tent by dig 30E.

It was Dr Cridget—his worn tweed jacket with ink stains on the sleeves, his peppery gray hair and big watery blue eyes. But it was Dr Cridget as Alister had never seen him before. He sat huddled on a camp bed, his knees up in his chest and his arms wrapped around them, as if he were afraid to let go for fear of being blown apart. He rocked back and forth on his seat, and a thin line of drool was slowly creeping down his chin.

"Cridget?" Alister said, advancing slowly. When there was no change in the poor man, he added: "Jeremy?"

Dr Cridget didn't seem to hear; he just sat there, rocking back and forth and sometimes jerking his head to one side, as if there were something in his ear he wanted to get out.

Gingerly Alister reached out and touched him on the shoulder.

"Jeremy, can you hear me?"

The effect was alarming: Dr Cridget jerked sideways, throwing himself against the wall of the tent, bringing his hands up to shield his face and kicking his legs out so wildly it was pure luck Alister wasn't struck. Then he began to make horrible gasping noises so far from human speech that it took Alister a moment to realize that was what it was.

"The *arms!*" cried Cridget, covering his face with his hands. "He has *terrible . . . aaarrms!*"

"Who has terrible arms?" Dr Carly asked, from a safe distance. "What did you *find*, Cridget?"

"He . . . will find *you!*" gasped Cridget, and went out like a light.

The Journal of Dr Alister Bane
Professor of Archeology, GTC, Oxford
June 11th 20- , 8:30 PM, Didcot dig, Oxfordshire

Unsettling day, my own problems notwithstanding. Dr Cridget is incomprehensible; he is drifting in and out of consciousness but when coaxed into speaking, he only wails about arms and an eye in the dark. We did manage to move him to the infirmary, which is a small mercy. So far as the poor man can feel things in this world, I believe he will be more comfortable there.

I had hoped to investigate the dig in question—30E— but the most astonishing thing had happened: it was flooded! The wretched intern overseeing it had noticed water creeping into the main chamber a little past noon but didn't say anything until the whole thing was flooded. We now have a system of pumps going, which should drain it by morning. Then Dr Carly and I will have a look for ourselves.

That night Alister dreamed of arms—long, twining green arms that held him fast and pulled him down, down, into a dark cold place. He was fighting against them, struggling to breathe, but he kept sinking. He was being dragged, inexorably, toward something sharp and terrible that would cut him open and leave him splayed out like an anatomy subject. The harder he fought the harder the arms gripped him, and there were more and more of them, sliding over him, curling around his neck . . .

Alister woke panting with sweat cooling on his brow and his bedroom an unfamiliar jumble of shadows before him. He had no memory of the dream, but he was left with the distinct feeling that he was in the wrong place; that the angle of the walls and the ceiling and the position of the window were all wrong, that the bed and the clothes were not his, that his whole life, in fact, belonged to someone else.

He got up and turned on the light, went into the bathroom and got a drink of water. By the time he went back to bed the feeling had passed, but he could not bring himself to turn off the light; it was still on when he woke later that morning, the sun shining full on his face.

The Journal of Dr Alister Bane
Professor of Archeology, GTC, Oxford
June 12th 20–, 9:00 AM, GTC, Oxford

The white flashes are becoming alarming. I had two more over breakfast, and they made me question whether I was well enough to to work today. But I know if I do not find out what happened to poor Cridget the curiosity will kill me.

As my tutor was so fond of telling me: knowledge is its own power and protection against our cruel world.

When Alister arrived at the dig Dr Carly met him at 30E, her face a mask of worry.

"What's the matter?" he asked before he was properly out of the van. "Did you find something?"

"It's what we haven't found that worries me," Dr Carly said. "Westing's gone missing."

"Westing?"

"Cridget's intern," said Dr Carly. "You remember, the one who let this thing get flooded in the first place? Well, she never reported in for work today. She's not at home and messages to her mobile get sent straight to voicemail. She was last seen here, checking the pumps last night."

"In 30E?" Alister asked, his heart sinking.

Carly glanced at the dark, wet hole that was the entrance to the fateful site. "Yes."

Alister shook his head. "We'll need full kit then," he said. "I'm not taking any chances."

Full kit meant body-suits, bagged feet, latex gloves and face masks. Alister also added a utility belt which carried a flashlight, small pickaxe, and a bag of vials for collecting samples. By the time he and Dr Carly entered site 30E a small crowd had gathered, and two brave interns—they had heard about Westing—had volunteered to accompany them.

They entered one at a time: Dr Carly first, then Alister, and finally the two interns—a spotty lad named Legston and a willowy girl called Punce.

30E had not been considered an important site, so the tunnel reaching down into the earth was fairly narrow—only wide enough for one person at a time. The shaft of Alister's flashlight caught on wet soil and supporting beams, and the ground was still covered in at least an inch of mud.

Finally the tunnel opened up, the steep walls reaching high above their heads to the dim gray of the tarpaulin that had been stretched over to keep the rain out. Here they stood in a square room of earth perhaps six feet on a side. The ground was a mess of sloppy mud, and the wall had been shored up in one place by planks of wood. It was otherwise empty.

Alister shook his head.

"Sample everything," he said, muffled through his mask.

As the two interns got to work, scraping dirt from the walls and scooping mud into little boxes, Alister probed about in the mud of the floor, searching for anything that might shed light on the situation.

The mud was clinging and tacky, and at one point he plunged his hand in too far, and his glove came loose as he pulled it free.

He felt the cool brush of the wet earth on his skin, but the next second it was *not* earth at all, but a long slimy tentacle the color of a green apple. It writhed up out of the sloppy muck, twining up and up around his arm until it had a firm hold. Then it *pulled.*

Alister found himself slammed into the mud face first, the interns' hands on him, Dr Carly speaking firmly in his ear:

"There, there, Dr B, you just breathe for me now. There must be a gas leak. We'll get you out and have this whole place scrubbed."

Alister found himself lifted clear of the mud—the tentacle had gone—and half led, half carried back up into the open air. Even as he reached the surface the world ran fluid before his eyes, and he was so frightened that it would flow completely away and leave him with nothing—or worse, whatever owned that tentacle—that he shut his eyes tight and refused to open them. The rest of his senses shut off soon after that.

Alister dreamed. He dreamed of a small, confined, dark place, where his body was held rigid and he was unable to move. He opened his mouth to scream—in horror? For help?—but instead of sound coming out, cold water rushed in. He choked on it, coughed; his lungs burned with the need for air and against all instinct he inhaled and—

And he woke up in a bland, uncomfortable camp bed, a metal framework supporting a fabric ceiling above his head.

"Why, *there* you are, Dr Bane," said a voice from over his shoulder, and he had another of those moments where he felt his entire life slide away from him, that he was someone else entirely, and that the bed, and the tent, and the entire world he was in was *not right*. He turned, slowly, trying not to dislodge the feeling yet at the same time desperately hoping it would go away.

A little round woman was sitting by his bedside, smiling at him from out of a halo of curly gray hair. Oddly, the first thing that went through Alister's mind was that her hair should have more color in it. But why would he think that? He had never seen this woman before in his life.

"Alister," said Alister. "My name is Alister."

"Of course it is, Dr Bane," said the woman. "Now you just lie back there, luv, and I'll have Dr Carly around to see you in just a mo. She's been in a right flutter over you." So saying the woman levered herself out of the chair she had been sitting in, her veined hands straining against the armrests. Brushing down her dress she looked about for her glasses, found them on the chain around her neck, put them on, and waddled sedately outside.

Alister lay back on his bed and tried to think logically. Clearly he had had some sort of episode, but was it related to the white flashes, or was it something different? It had not felt like those jerks out of reality he had experienced before; those had simply been neurons misfiring and making him think he saw one thing in place of another. Like the feeling of *deja vu*, it had only been a matter of signals getting a bit out of order. This was a full-on hallucination.

Gingerly, Alister raised the arm that had been assaulted, and peeled back the sleeve. To his horror he found the skin raised and reddened, with white circular marks embedded in his flesh. They were just the right size, and spaced just so, to have been made by the suckers that underlined the tentacle that had grabbed him.

There was a rustle outside the tent and the sound of approaching feet, and impulsively Alister pulled down his sleeve to cover the marks.

"Good to see you, Dr B," said Dr Carly, pushing aside the flap of tarpaulin that was serving as a door. "You had us right worried there for a while."

Alister found he was thrusting his arm under the cover as if the marks were something shameful he needed to hide. The little gray-haired nurse was back, peering around Carly's elbow with cheerful curiosity. To his relief Carly noticed her, and at a quiet word she vanished.

"What happened?" he asked, once the nurse was safely gone.

"I was hoping you could tell me that," Carly said, sitting down in the wobbly camp chair. "You keeled over like someone had pummeled you, and when we finally dragged you upright you went out like a light."

"How long?" Alister rubbed his eyes.

"Nearly four hours," Dr Carly said.

Alister lay back on his bed and regarded the ceiling thought-fully. Four hours wasn't bad, not really, not as bad as losing a day, or a week, or not waking up at all. But he still felt cheated, like there had been a chunk of his life that had been stolen away, and he would never get it back.

"And," said Carly, reaching into her pocket, "we found this clutched in your hand. Mind telling us where you got it?"

She produced a small rectangular chip of plastic, the size and shape of the sort of flash drive for the older digital cameras. Al-ister took it with his good hand and brought it close for a better look. There appeared to be something drawn on it, a circle with ten wavy rays shooting out of it and a single dot in its center.

Something like memory slammed hard into Alister's brain. For one moment he *knew* he had seen this pictograph before. The image of a door with this same drawing on it swam before his eyes, and behind that door was—

Alister noticed his vision going white around the edges. Quickly he curled his hand around the chip and pushed it away under the covers. Then he had to lie very still with his eyes shut while Dr Carly put her head out of the tent and called the nurse back in. He wished she hadn't. Alister felt like he could confide in Dr Carly, but not with the nurse there. If he started talking about white flashes and hallucinations he knew they would ship him off to infirmary, and then he would *never* get this mystery solved.

It came as something of a surprise to realize that he *wanted* to solve this mystery at all, that he had begun to look at the whole mess like one of his archeological problems. There was missing data here, and he had to either dig for more, or content himself with connecting the dots. Since the dots in this case were strung so far apart it would take impossible leaps to connect them, he realized he would have to do more digging.

At least now I know what poor Cridget meant by "terrible arms," he thought to himself as the nurse checked his vitals. The uncomfortable thought that perhaps Cridget had had a similar experience, and that Alister's mind was on its way to breaking just like his had, floated up to the surface, but Alister stuffed it back down again.

"I'm *fine*," he said, a little more forcefully than he intended, sitting up abruptly and swinging his legs over the side of the bed.

This was a mistake. The natural dynamics of gravity on a body with low blood pressure swung into effect, and Alister was hit by another bout of dizziness—though this was the normal kind of dizziness brought on by standing up too fast, and it soon passed. Having something to compare his white-outs and hallucinations to made him able to look at the situation much more clinically. Obviously something unnatural was going on here, and he needed to find out what.

"I don't fancy you're fine enough to get home on your own," Dr Carly said, laying a steadying hand on his shoulder and gently pushing him back down.

"There must be a gas pocket we're disturbing," he said, casting about for some semblance of a rational explanation. "Better have that area cordoned off before we continue digging. Now get me those two interns, I want to hear their side of the story."

Dr Carly pursed her lips, but she disappeared out of the tent, taking the little nurse with her. Alister was left alone with his thoughts—which were not much of a comfort—for almost an hour. In that time he went from nervous and restless, to bored, to increasingly nervous as the time stretched on and no one entered the tent.

At last there was some shuffling and not Dr Carly, nor the little gray haired nurse, but another intern entered. The interns were indistinguishable to Alister's eyes, but he got the impression this was a new one. The boy had a freckled face and an unfortunate mop of red hair. He coughed.

"Professor Bane?" he said.

"Do you see anyone else here?" Alister asked testily.

"Yes sir, I mean, no sir," said the intern, clapping his hands behind his back and shuffling his feet nervously. "Only, Dr Carly sent me to tell you they can't find them. They are looking hard, sir, only it's—" he chewed his lip furiously, and an idea oozed into Alister's mind, uncomfortable and cold.

"They're gone, aren't they?" he said.

"Legs and Punce haven't been seen for *hours!*" wailed the intern, the dam of nerves breaking in a torrent of sobs. "I *saw* them go into the de-con tent, but *they never came out.* No one's seen them since. They're not at home or answering their mobiles, they've *gone*—just like Westing!"

Just like Westing, who let the dig get flooded and then had to check the pumps. The cold pushed forward through Alister's mind like an advancing wave of slime, and he found himself clutching his forehead involuntarily.

"I'm sorry sir," stammered the new intern. "I'll try harder to find them."

"No, you won't," Alister said from behind his hand. "You're going to take me to the archive."

"Sir?"

"You have a car, don't you?"

"I could borrow Gordon's . . . "

"Then do so," Alister said, rising slowly to his feet.

The archive was located in the basement of the Bodleian, renovated a few years back to contain banks and banks of digital storage. It was cold down in the archive, and Alister was wishing he'd had the intern stop by the GTC to get an extra coat, or scarf, or both, as he zipped through page after page of scanned manuscript. He was attempting to put together a history of the site of the Didcot dig through the centuries, but was hampered by the fact that, for the better part of the last few thousand years, it had been nothing more than a nondescript field.

Flick. Flick. Flick. The pages flashed across the screen. Then . . . *flick.* A blank page with *"Archive not scanned, please see hardcopy"* in the middle. Alister cursed under his breath.

"Gilthwait?" he called, trying to keep the frustration out of his voice.

The intern appeared from around a corner of computer stacks, his coat buttoned up under his chin. "Sir?" he said.

"Gilthwait, would you go up to . . . " Alister squinted at the header of the page, which listed the location of the hardcopy. " . . . Historical Archive, row 36B, and bring me down all the annals that could have anything on Didcot?"

Gilthwait paled. "All of them sir?"

"I said all," Alister snapped.

Without a word, Gilthwait vanished. Alister turned back to the screen.

The intern was gone a long time. A *very* long time. In the end Alister lost patience and climbed back upstairs himself. He was getting hungry, not a state that lent itself well to careful, analytical thinking.

He did not find Gilthwait. He did find the section he was looking for, however, and concluded that the wretched youth had taken the opportunity to scamper off. Sighing to himself he went along the shelves, picking off books and scanning their indexes.

Pick, shuffle, replace. Pick, shuffle, replace. Pick, shuffle, replace. Pause. Pick back up again. Slowly Alister reopened the book and stared at what he found there. Or rather, what he *didn't* find there.

The book *said* it contained facsimiles of land deeds going back as far as the twelfth century, but the pages inside . . . were *perfectly blank.*

Alister stared at them, willing the ink to appear. Instead all he got was the uncomfortable cold feeling in his mind, like slime seeping in between the cracks.

Hastily he shoved that book away and picked up the next.

It was blank.

And the next . . .

Blank.

The rest of the shelf was nothing but blank books. In desperation Alister picked up one of the earlier books he had already dismissed.

Arms—green, boneless, writhing arms—exploded out of the book at him. They reached out, twined around his head, pulled his face down into the book. Cold, sticky slime hit his face, ran up his nose, into his mouth when he opened it in surprise. It tasted faintly of something like whiskey, and something else that made him retch.

Keep looking.

The words felt like they were being written on his brain with acid. They burned. Painful to think about; impossible to forget.

Keep looking in the cracks.

The voice belonged to a mind that was old and deep and stretched out around him into infinite space. Alister knew he would dissolve into that space if it went on much longer . . .

As suddenly as the horrible arms had appeared, they vanished. Perhaps they retreated into the pages of the book, perhaps they were pulled away into some other dimension. All Alister knew was suddenly he could breathe again, he could open his eyes and see again—though his mouth still tasted vaguely foul.

Slowly he closed the book, replaced it on the shelf. He walked composedly to the end of the row, down the stairs to the common area where he found a vacant table and sat down, pulling out his journal. With a hand that shook only a little he began to write.

The Journal of Dr Alister Bane
Professor of Archeology, GTC, Oxford
June 12th 20–, 6:05 PM, Bodleian Library

Either there is something very wrong with me, or very wrong with the world. Reason and logic tell me the fault must lie within my own mind, but something else tells me this may not be so. The disappearances of the interns—Westing, Legston and Punce. Gilthwait may have run off, but in light of recent events I doubt I will see him again.

Where have they gone? Will they ever return? Has the world broken to such a degree that people are slipping through the cracks?

Cracks.

I must look in the cracks. I must find answers.

Am I going mad? I must certainly be mad if I think the world is breaking and not just my own mind. Perhaps it is my mind after all . . .

No! No! There is something in my gut that tells me there is more wrong than just what I can perceive. There is something at work here: an intelligence far greater than anything we have yet encountered. An extraterrestrial? That is one hypothesis. But how to *test* it?

Alister paused in his writing, absently chewing at the end of his pen. A few students had come into the room, and they were talking animatedly amongst themselves.

" . . . which it *wasn't* blank when Professor McBride assigned it to me last week," one of them, a girl, said.

Alister pricked up his ears and listened, straining to hear over the pounding of his heart.

"You sure this isn't a prank?" her friend, a dark girl with a cloth over her hair, replied.

"Oh sure, because anyone can swap the right number of blank pages—pages made of *perfectly aged paper*—with the *exact same* cover I've had in my room all week," said the first girl, whose hair was dyed an improbable shade of pink.

Alister stared, his mind in a whirl. Not least over what was being said, but the image of a woman with pink hair was pushing forward in his mind. She was familiar, frightening, but also somehow reassuring. Alister was desperately trying to place her even as he rose to his feet and made his way through the tables towards the two girls. They saw him approach and fell silent in the presence of what was clearly a don, and a possibly deranged one, to judge from the way he was staring.

"Excuse me," Alister began, and realized he had lost the image of the pink-haired woman. All he saw before him now was a girl of about twenty with a cheap dye job and freckles over her cheeks. He gave himself an internal shake, and said: "I overheard you expressing dismay over your predicament. May I see the offending book?"

The student raised an eyebrow, but she shuffled through her bag and eventually brought out a truly ancient tome with crinkled, yellow pages. Taking it in both hands Alister opened it carefully.

The pages were all quite blank.

Turning back to the cover he saw it was an obscure history of the Norman conquest.

"When did you notice this?" he asked.

"This morning," replied the student nervously. "Am I going to be in very much trouble?"

"Not with me," Alister said, handing the book back. "But if you find any more of your history books going blank, do give me a ring." He gave her his card and departed, leaving the two young women staring dumbstruck at his retreating back.

Alister stood in the cooling air outside the library, breathing deep the smell of the city: of car exhaust and dirty stones and the enticing smell of frying meat that was slowly wafting up from Oxford's many restaurants. His stomach growled, and he realized with a jolt that he had not eaten since breakfast. Quickly he hobbled into the nearest pub and sat down, leaning back against the creaking leather seat and closing his eyes.

He ordered, and when the food came he ate it ravenously, so fast he barely tasted it, but the empty feeling inside him was sated, and he could think clearly once more.

He walked home slowly through the late summer evening— the sky still bright blue and pink above him, while the buildings all around had fallen into shadow. But it now seemed a false image to him: a thin film stretched over a dark abyss, into which he would fall if ever the surface cracked.

Why did that seem familiar? It shouldn't. His whole life had been dedicated to studying the history of the world; he knew the ways of it better than most; these thoughts and feelings should be alien to him.

Alister walked faster, rushing through the gates of GTC without answering the porter's cheerful, "Good evening Professor Bane," and up the steps to his rooms, a cold sweat breaking out on his brow.

There were a number of messages on his phone, mostly from Dr Carly worrying about him, a couple from his students. Alister let the tape play without really listening to what the recorded voices were telling him. He made himself a cup of tea and while it steeped went into the bathroom to wash his face.

Standing in front of the sink, running a soft cloth over his face, he felt the prick of stubble on his chin. He had neglected to shave that morning; would have to shave tomorrow. He peered into the mirror to get an idea of the situation, and froze.

The face that stared back at him from the glass was *all wrong*. There were bags under his eyes and lines at their corners and across his cheeks. His hair was too short, too light—he realized it was light because there was so much gray in it. It should be darker—*had* been darker, he was certain. He felt his heart jump as he realized he could not remember the last time he had seen a picture of himself.

He tore through his apartment, searching for albums, snapshots, keepsakes—anything that was likely to have his photograph on them. The picture on his photo ID was the same face as the one in the mirror, and though it said "ALISTER BANE, D.O.B. June 28 1964" that also struck him as somehow wrong.

There were no albums. All the framed photographs on his desk and mantel were postcards of Oxford. It was as though he had never lived anywhere else—had never been anything else—than a professor of archeology at one of the colleges of Oxford University.

Which was ridiculous. He had plenty of memories. Growing up in Scotland with his grandparents. Learning to ride a bicycle. Making mobiles of the solar system to hang in his room when he was twelve.

Not so long ago, but very far away, a voice burned in the back of his head.

Alister fled to the bathroom, gripping the edges of the sink and pressing his eyes closed, willing that when he opened them the face that looked back at him would be the *right* one. Not this gray and worn stranger. But aside from his skin being whiter, and his eyes being wider, his face looked the same as before: *wrong*.

"Bloody *hells!*" Alister cursed, and slammed his fist into the glass.

There was a cracking sound, and white hot pain shot up his arm. Alister recoiled, hoping the cracking had been the glass of the mirror, and not his bones. He stood, nursing his throbbing hand, until the pain gently ebbed away. There was blood from a dark cut on the side of his palm, and looking up he saw the mirror had indeed cracked: a perfect three-way break that fractured into a spiderweb near the center. Now there were three broken images of the wrong face looking back at him, but Alister was no longer looking at them. He was staring at the dark space between the fragments; at the cracks in the glass.

Don't be afraid to look in the cracks . . .

Alister leaned forward, still cradling his injured hand.

It was not only darkness behind the glass; there was something that moved in it, fluid and graceful, like a fish through water. Alister pressed up against the cold porcelain of the sink, peering closer.

Something flashed in the dark; something gold and orange that blinked at him. An eye. A giant eye. A trickle of thick green slime oozed out of the crack and down the glass. The glass was bleeding—bleeding green slime. Strangely, Alister felt possessed of the urgent need to touch it.

"Don't, Dr Bane!" A voice rang out behind him. It broke whatever spell had been cast over his mind, and Alister recoiled from the dripping, broken mirror.

The little gray-haired nurse stood in the doorway, clutching at the walls and red in the face. She pushed herself forward into the room, grabbed Alister by the elbow, and pulled him away—

out. She slammed the door behind them, but not before Alister saw the mirror erupt as countless green tentacles exploded into the room.

"What—that—thing—you can *see* it?"   Alister gasped. "What *is* it?!"

"I can't explain," the little woman said, putting her back to the door even as it jumped under her shoulders. Slime began to ooze around the cracks, staining the floor a lurid green.

"Perhaps you remember stories of monsters?"   she said. "This is a monster. An old, *strong* monster. It doesn't belong here. It's from a world I can't imagine—one *couldn't*—imagine without going mad. But it's coming. It's coming for *you* Dr Bane. It wants *you*."

There was a crash, and a particularly large tentacle thrust its way through the door, groping.

Alister had so many questions he wanted to ask: how did the nurse know? How had she gotten into his apartment? But those questions were wiped away as the terrible arm, dripping slime, puckers sucking horribly, wound its way around the old woman's waist.

"You'll have to run, Dr Bane," she whispered. Then shouted: "Run, run, *run!*" The last word became a scream, which became a wail, which was finally choked off as the arm found her mouth and plunged into it, tearing clean through her throat. Red blood mixed with the brilliant green slime, and splinters of the door went everywhere as dozens more tentacles burst through, ripping at her body and burrowing deep.

Alister slipped in something—blood or slime or both, he didn't know—as he ran from the room. He made it to the bottom of the stairs before he had to stop and empty his stomach onto the bottom step.

Outside the night was finally closing in, but the world was far from going quiet. It was filled with sound. The sound, Alister realized with a sick jolt, of people screaming.

On shaking legs he handed himself along the wall of the college to the deserted porter's gate. The railing there had been smashed in, twisted around on itself . . . and it was dripping in green slime. Beyond, in the street, the buildings opposite the college were lit from behind by an angry orange light. A fire.

Somewhere Oxford was burning, but there were no sirens, no honks, no sounds of traffic. What there was were the sounds of pounding feet, and as Alister picked his way carefully through the destroyed gate he saw a bedraggled crowd of people hurrying up the street. They were heading for the center of town, away from the canal, and many of them looked slick and shiny. Wet, dripping. As he reached the street a girl slipped and fell in front of him, her hair dark from the slime running down her back, but still vividly pink. The girl from the library. The girl with the blank book.

Alister stared at her dumbly for a second, then reached down and hauled her to her feet. There were more people hurrying up the street now, some on the pavement and some in the road, and they would have been trampled if Alister had not begun pushing forward.

"Steady now," he said, though he felt anything but.

"It got—" the girl gasped. "It got *Mally!*" she sobbed, tripping over her own toes. "She went to *pieces!*"

"I can imagine," Alister said grimly. The adrenaline and fear had curled into a tight knot in his stomach, settling into a ball that, far from causing him to panic, acted as a sort of anchor. His world narrowed to just the essentials: keep the girl safe, get away from what was coming.

People were pushing past them now, and Alister hooked an arm around the girl's elbow and hurried them on. But her arm kept slipping—it was covered in that thing's slime—and when he turned to readjust it he felt his other hand slide clean through, as though she were made of butter or warm gelatin. For one moment he met her eyes—wide and terrified and tear-filled—and then she dissolved into a puddle of lumpish slime.

Alister stopped, letting the traffic of people push around him. He stared back down the road to where the sky was lit from below with a warm yellow light, and for a moment he thought he saw, silhouetted against the firmament, the shadow of a great curling arm.

A tall man in a long black coat knocked into him as he went hurrying by. Alister noticed because, unlike the rest of the crowd, this man did not seem at all panicked. He walked swiftly, purposefully, but without anxiety. As though he were merely in a hurry to catch a train. The sight of his contained figure moving through the screaming crowd jolted Alister's brain back into action. He made himself turn and follow in the man's wake. People got out of the way for this man without seeming to notice, and in the ebb that flowed behind him Alister broke into a run. He followed all the way past the graveyard at St. Giles before the man made a sudden jerking move to one side, and vanished into the crowd.

Alister stumbled on a loose brick. He fell to his hands as the road trembled beneath him, and the screams behind him redoubled. There was a deafening crunching sound, and the ground beneath him began to sink. Craning his head over his shoulder, Alister saw a giant sinkhole forming in the middle of Woodstock Road. The people who had been behind him were already tumbling down into it, and Alister was perched precariously on its edge.

The ground below him heaved. He began to slide backward . . .

A thin withered hand closed around his, and he turned to find his rescuer was . . . was . . .

The little gray-haired nurse, whole and unbloodied and very much alive, looked back at him along her deceptively strong arm.

"You—what—" Alister began.

"No time for questions!" the nurse shouted at him over the crashing of stone and plaster as the houses on either side began to collapse. Her voice was no longer cracked and old, but rich and musical, with a strange accent.

Alister hesitated.

It was a fatal mistake.

The ground dropped out from under him and he fell, clutching at the jagged earth, one hand still gripped by the nurse.

She might yet have saved him, might have drawn on that mysterious strength and pulled him up to safety, but then a cool tendril of clammy muscle wrapped around Alister's ankle. He did not have to look to know that one of the arms had grabbed him.

He opened his mouth to speak, to scream, but an arm looped over his chest and constricted, pushing the air out of him in a wheeze.

The old woman grimaced, showing her yellow teeth, and clung to his hand even harder. Alister thought his bones would break, or she'd rip his hand clean off.

He wanted her to let go. He was finished: done. The terror of that filled him like a bitter fire, but behind that was the icy chill of despair.

He wanted her to hold on. To save him—somehow! Anyhow! He did not want to die now.

In the end he did not have a choice. Another arm, slender and tinged yellow, slithered up his own to where the woman gripped his hand. The tentacle was slick with slime, glistening in the light of the distant fire. The very end of it curled, almost gently, around the woman's wrist, and went through it like a red-hot wire through butter. It came smoothly off the end of her arm, and Alister felt the earth beneath his fingers begin to slide past as he was dragged down.

Rocks jolted him, and broken pieces of concrete scratched at him. He saw the sky encircled by the rim of the sinkhole, and then one of the tentacles closed over his eyes. The world went dark as he was pulled under water, the cold stinging against his bare skin. He felt the pressure building against him as those arms—those terrible, terrible arms, pulled him down into the abyss.

This is how it ends, he thought, stunned with terror as he felt a tentacle press against his mouth.

And then, in the dark and the cold, burning on his mind like acid, a voice said:

No, it isn't.

Part Two

A LISTER WAS COLD—freezing cold—and there was something horrible in his mouth. It was hard and slippery, and it choked him. He tried to cough, tried to reach up and pull it out, and discovered that he couldn't feel his arms. Couldn't feel the rest of his body, for that matter.

Then there was air in his lungs—sweet, blessed air! And it was being forced out of him, and that horrible tube with it. It felt like the worst coughing fit from the worst cold he'd ever had, but then it was gone and he could take a breath. He became aware of his lungs and diaphragm, pumping air in and out. He tried to open his eyes, but they seemed glued shut.

Something damp and warm was pressed against his face, wiping away the gluey slime, and he opened his eyes.

Round golden-brown cat eyes stared back at him out of a perfectly smooth, hairless face, which was framed in a halo of pink hair—a wig, Alister knew.

The face smiled, showing bright white, square teeth.

"Hello Mr Alister," said Professor Odd. "*Welcome back.*"

Alister stared at her groggily. His mind was a jumble of memories. He seemed to have two sets: one of a life in Oxford, and another of a life that involved a ship that travelled between universes, a talking dog, giant flying whales, robots—and Professor Odd.

Professor Odd, who had a flesh-colored tentacle arm dotted with green leopard spots growing out the back of her head. Who had jaguar eyes and a sword cane with a silver banana for a handle—or had she given that away? The more recent memories from that set were a little fuzzy, as if they had been smudged over and were only now coming back into focus.

"What . . . happened?" Alister rasped. His mouth felt like paper and his throat was so dry he could barely swallow.

"You were trapped," the Professor explained gently. "But we got you out."

"I can't feel . . . " Alister began, craning his head around so he could get a look at his body, just to reassure himself that it was still there.

He appeared to be naked, covered only by a thin white sheet—which explained why he was so cold—out of which he could just see his toes poking at the other end. Also emerging from under the sheet was an alarming tangle of tubes and wires, and he could hear the faint hum of a pump nearby.

"Relax," said Professor Odd, laying a soothing hand on his shoulder. "You did well. You can rest now."

Alister did not want to rest. He wanted to get away from those tubes. He wanted to get warm. He was also, in a distant but fast-approaching way, very hungry.

"You can put him out now, Dave," Professor Odd said to something behind Alister's head. "He doesn't need to feel this."

Alister's eyes flew open as he felt something small and soft and smooth and wet curl around his left ear. After the first flush of terror, he realized it seemed timid, gentle as a cat's tail as it wriggled inside. That tickled a little, and Alister would have laughed except he couldn't get his diaphragm to work properly.

"Dave," he said, smiling foggily up at Professor Odd's face. "It was *Dave* the whole time . . . "

Inside his head he felt the words appear, soft like rain in dust.

Yes, they said. *It was me.*

Alister Bane went out like a light.

When next Alister woke he was warm, lying on his side with something soft and fuzzy under his cheek. He was aware of his feet, deliciously warm, and he curled his toes to make sure they still worked. Then he slowly worked his way up, flexing his legs, his back, his fingers, his arms. Finally he cracked his eyes open and looked around.

He appeared to be lying on and under a pile of sheets, a few inches from a wall made of bits of metal bolted together. Alister lay there and tried to sort through his memories.

He was twenty-two (or thereabouts; it was hard to tell after his time aboard the Oddity), not *fifty-two*. He had been to university at Redfair, not Oxford. Had Redfair even existed in that other world? And the Old Country was called *Alba,* not Scotland.

And Dave was not a giant Cthulian monster bent on destroying the world. He was the size of a pie plate, had only ten arms, and as far as Alister knew, had never shown the slightest inclination towards violence.

Still, all his memories from that other place, that false world, were disturbingly vivid. He could remember the sight of the poor old woman being ripped to pieces, and half-expected to find scratches and bruises on his chest and hands—leftovers from a pointless struggle.

Light was coming in from over his shoulder, and as his eyes adjusted to the glow he began to roll over—becoming aware as he did so of odd aches and pains, some in alarmingly intimate places. His hands, when he examined them, were free of new injuries, though he could feel the rough skin of old scabs over his knuckles. *From climbing out of the canyon in the impossible world,* he remembered with some relief. Now he thought about it, he found more memories from the recent past unfurling around him.

They had been discussing the differences in time between universes: him, the Professor, Dave and Elo. Professor Odd had explained how related universes did not advance in synch with each other. There were temporally retarded universes that, if you visited them now, would appear very much like Alister's home world *had* two hundred years ago. Similarly, there were temporally advanced universes that *had been* exactly like Alister's—but were now hundreds or even thousands of years in what he would call the future. Professor Odd explained that Elo came from just such a universe.

"AND ME." Dave interjected through his translator. They had all looked at him curiously: Dave had not been forthcoming with information about where he was from, or even how he had wound up in Alister's universe posing as a student in the first place, and none of them had felt comfortable asking. Now they waited expectantly, but Dave said no more.

Eventually Alister had asked if this meant these universes told the future.

Professor Odd had shrugged. "One possible future of many. There's no guarantee that your universe will develop along any one predetermined path, because there's an awful lot of randomness and chaos involved—which of course is what makes it so much fun."

Alister had asked if they could visit one of these future universes.

"Temporally *advanced*," Elo had corrected him. "Remember, to them, it's the *present*, and *you're* from the past."

"Then how do you decide which universes are retarded, which ones are advanced, and which ones are normal?" Alister asked a little testily.

"It's a matter of averages," Professor Odd had said. "The great majority of related universes—that is, universes that share a common history—are at about the same time. But you have outliers, universes that are *behind* or *ahead* of the pack. You, for example, come from a universe that is nearly at the center of this normal range. I come from one that's a little ahead, and Elo—and Dave—come from universes that are forward outliers."

Alister had asked again if they could visit one.

"Certainly," said Professor Odd with a grin. "Elo, I promised you a visit home, didn't I?"

Elo made a face. "I'm not sure that would be a good idea. Humans still aren't widely accepted in my world."

Professor Odd had shrugged. "Well, that leaves us half an infinite number to choose from," she had said cheerfully, and went over to the Oddity's cockpit to scan for worlds.

As he recalled these events, Alister groaned. It had been *his fault* they ended up . . . wherever *this* was. *Whenever* this was. He brought up a hand to rub at his face.

His skin felt . . . smooth. Too smooth. Where he should have felt at least a little stubble there was just skin, and instead of the tufts of his eyebrows, all he felt were hairless ridges. Moving on and up, he felt the shape of his skull, shaved as clean as the Professor's.

"*Son* of a—" Alister exclaimed, shooting up into a sitting position.

Down at his feet, something warm and furry stirred, sat up, and glared at him.

"If you say 'bitch' I won't be your foot-warmer anymore," Elo said irritably. "Count yourself lucky."

Elo was naked. Which was to say she wore nothing but her normally thick coat of golden fur. Except now there was a conspicuous bald patch on the back of her head between her ears—it reminded Alister of how vets shaved the legs of cats and dogs before giving them I.V.s. Elo looked like a golden wolf that had been attacked by a team of these vets; now he looked, he saw similar bald patches around her neck, and—yes—on her legs.

"Elo," he said. "What happened to you?"

"The same thing that happened to you," Elo said, lying back down with one foreleg draped over his shin.

Alister swallowed uneasily. "And . . . what . . . what was that?"

Elo twitched an ear. "You don't remember?"

Alister shook his head sadly. "I remember the discussion we had about advanced universes," he said. "I take it we found one?"

"Oh yes, we did," Elo said soberly. She was about to say more, when there was a rattling from above, and Professor Odd dropped out of the ceiling.

To be precise, she dropped out of a hatch in the ceiling, but to Alister's still groggy brain it looked as though she had magically appeared.

She landed face-first on all fours with a heavy *"Oof!"* then rolled into a sitting position and rubbed her hands. She was still wearing the same bright pink wig and green trenchcoat, and now in addition she had on a little canvas backpack. This she slung off her shoulders even as she leaned forward and craned her neck to call back up through the hole.

"You're clear, Dave. Come *on.*"

Alister looked up—and felt his mouth open in amazement.

The hatch in the ceiling which he had first taken to be an air duct of some kind in fact opened onto a tilted view of the Oddity. He got the strangest feeling of being in one place, looking up into another where the direction of gravity had been rotated about ninety degrees. For instead of the ceiling of the Oddity, he found himself looking at the little stairs leading up, and beyond that the distant lights of the cockpit, and beyond that the hulking shape of the cluttered table.

Dave was sitting on the bottom stair in his panvironment suit, seeming to magically hover in the ceiling, obviously still affected by the Oddity's gravity, and not the outer universe's. Then, even as Alister watched, he rolled forward the last few crucial inches, and plummeted out of the ceiling, landing with a hard *clang* on the floor.

The noise jogged some of Alister's memories. He remembered that drop: stepping through the door and feeling gravity rotate around him. It had nearly made him sick.

Mostly, however, Alister felt a huge wave of relief crashing over him. They had the Oddity. They could *escape*.

Professor Odd approached him and set the backpack down at his side.

"Feeling better, Mr Alister?" she asked.

"Much," said Alister. The prospect of leaving this strange and terrifying place had done wonders for him.

"Good," said the Professor cheerfully. "Now get dressed. We have work to do."

Alister found to his consternation that he was wearing only a flimsy white robe, not unlike a hospital gown. Professor Odd and Elo held up one of the sheets as a modesty curtain while he climbed into the clothes that had been in the backpack. (A pair of red corduroy trousers, an electric blue shirt with yellow stars, matching red corduroy jacket, mercifully white underwear and socks, and pink cowboy boots.)

"Sorry about the selection," Professor Odd said from behind the sheet. "It was what the Oddity had on top, and I didn't think you'd want to wait."

Alister paused with one boot half on. If they were simply going to escape into the Oddity, why bother bringing him clothes in the first place?

"Professor?" Alister said, shoving his foot down into the boot. "What are we going to do?"

"WE ARE GOING," answered Dave, "TO FINISH WHAT WE STARTED."

"Started?" Alister echoed. He ripped the sheet down and glared at Dave. "What exactly did we *start?*"

Professor Odd gazed at him. She seemed surprised. "Oh dear," she said. "It got in deep, didn't it? How much do you remember?"

"I remember we were discussing future—*temporally advanced worlds*—and I asked if we could visit one, and you said yes. I remember falling through that door." He pointed up. "And then . . . "

Then there was a confusion of darkness and noises, a pain in his head, and then blackness. Alister didn't feel up to describing it, so he just waved his hand vaguely.

"And now I have this second set of memories, like from another life, where I was a professor in Oxford and . . . " he jerked to a stop, one of those memories swimming to the surface; a large yellow dog that pushed a note into his hand. "*You* were there," he said, rounding on Elo.

"We *all* were," said Professor Odd, sitting down on the hard metal floor and crossing her legs. She patted the floor beside her. "Come, sit. I'll explain everything. Do you think you could manage some food?"

Alister did. He took the little white container and spoon Professor Odd offered and sat beside her. It was yogurt, and it was cold, and it sat in his stomach like a rock, but it was far better than the emptiness he had been feeling. And while he ate, Professor Odd explained.

"We are on Earth. Your planet," she said. "But it's a version of Earth over fifty thousand years ahead of yours. On this Earth, humans evolved along much the same lines as your world. Here, they developed technology to start *and stop* global warming, to start *and stop* several mass extinctions, and several world wars. They did not develop enough, however, to alter the Earth's natural warming and cooling cycle. In your world, you live in the middle of one of Earth's temperate periods—without human interference, it would begin to cool down again in, oh, twenty thousand years, and enter another ice age. That is what happened here: this world is now at the *end* of that ice age, with the glaciers receding and sea levels rising and the flora and fauna reshuffling themselves to adapt to the new world."

Alister nodded. He was getting the itchy feeling in his brain that the Professor had told him all this before—used these exact words, even. But he couldn't place the memory, so he remained silent and listened.

"Meanwhile, the humans have been hibernating," she went on. "You see, they *did* develop the technology to put their bodies into suspended animation, and the better part of the population of this Earth has waited out the long cold underground—where we are now. But they didn't just put themselves under, these humans—oho *no*—they built—"

"They built a *machine!*" Alister exclaimed, and the memories came flooding back.

A machine the size of France, stretched out across the North African desert like a giant starfish, under the ground where Egypt, Sudan and Chad had once been. Alister distinctly remembered the Professor showing him an old satellite picture where the lines of the machine were visible as points of light.

That had been in the Archive, he remembered. The Archive was a narrow rift along the southeastern arm, riddled with pockets and traversable by a complex system of carts and cables that had reminded Alister of a particularly frustrating puzzle game. Within the pockets were viewing screens with strange-looking keyboards that had taken the Professor almost an hour to figure out, but once she did, the information they had uncovered had been astounding.

At first they had thought what they'd stumbled into was some sort of underground bunker to allow humans to wait out the cold. Then they realized it was much more than that.

It was a time capsule. A stasis locker. Closer to the surface, instead of stored information, there were stored human beings. Rack upon rack of them, packed like sardines, each in its own little life-support pod, each wired into a network of cables that ran between the pods, twining toward the center of the starfish where they coalesced into one giant computer.

"It's a *dream machine*," Professor Odd had whispered in wonder.

"A *what?*" Alister had said.

"A machine for dreaming." The Professor turned to him with wide eyes. "Their bodies are in suspended animation, but their minds are all active—and *interacting with each other.* That's what this machine does: it creates a mental landscape for the minds of those hard-wired into it to interact with each other."

Alister had blinked in astonishment. "You mean, like in *The Matrix?*"

"I never finished that movie," Professor Odd said absently, turning back to the screen. "They highly underestimated the power of a biological brain in a constructed reality. It was annoying." She began typing away. "What I want to know . . . " she continued under her breath, " . . . is what it's *doing* with their minds. Is it a paradise? A live reconstruction of the outside world? Are there children . . . ?"

The computer that accessed the information in the Archive and displayed it on the screen operated by a very simple set of commands. Professor Odd typed in the command on the keyboard, and the computer obeyed. But after four or five more requests for information the computer began *asking questions.*

"*Who are you?*" was written on the screen after Professor Odd had requested a detailed description of the virtual world created by the machine.

She had stared at the question for some time, then written back:

"*I am Professor Odd. Who are you?*"

The computer didn't answer. Instead it asked another question.

"*What are you doing here?*"

"*Exploring,*" typed the Professor. "*Who are you?*"

"*What do you want?*"

Professor Odd regarded the screen, a little crease forming between her nonexistent brows.

"*I want you to tell me who/what you are.*"

In the distance, Alister had heard a faint humming sound and had assumed it was just a fan kicking on. Dave had known better, he now realized. The creature had trundled off to the nearest cart and disappeared into the lower levels of the archive while they still waited for the computer's answer.

Finally the words flashed on the screen, almost too fast for Alister to read:

"I am the Elder."

And then the power had gone out.

Alister jerked out of his reverie and looked up at Professor Odd, and Elo, who crouched over him. They were in one of the upper alcoves of the Archive, he now remembered. He could see Dave sitting in the doorway. Keeping watch. Standing guard.

"It got us, didn't it?" he said, nervously running a hand over his smooth head. "All that stuff in Oxford, me being an archeologist . . . that was all inside the machine. *That's* what it's doing to the human minds: replaying history."

Professor Odd nodded. "It got you quick, then me and Elo when we tried to rescue you." She pulled a distasteful face.

"It was embarrassing," Elo said. "It thought I was a regular *dog.* Plugged me in with all the non-human animals—did you know there's practically a zoo on the lower levels?"

"And then the machine made a mistake," Professor Odd said, her eyes gleaming.

"It got *Dave,*" Elo said.

Professor Odd sat down next to Alister and explained.

"This machine was made for human minds. You are human, I function as a human, Elo has human-level intelligence. Our biology was compatible with its hardware, and it was able to integrate our minds into its virtual world with more or less success. But *Dave,*" she glanced along to the panvironment suit sitting in the doorway, "Dave isn't even *remotely* human—mentally or biologically. He doesn't even have what we would recognize as a brain. So even though the machine managed to get him *in,* it couldn't control him once he *was* in. He got me and Elo out in a jiffy, but you were a little more difficult. You were in *deep.*"

"I remember seeing Elo," Alister said. He looked up at her. "You were the dog in the graveyard. You gave me that note: *don't be afraid to look in the cracks.*"

Elo nodded gravely. "The machine's virtual reality isn't perfect. If we could get your mind to start picking up on the little problems, the inconsistencies, then it would be easier to extract you."

Alister laughed weakly. "It didn't work."

"Oh, but it *did,*" Professor Odd insisted. "Think back, Alister. Did you ever have flashes of *this is wrong,* or *I don't belong here?*"

Alister thought back, and had to admit that he had. "I didn't know what to make of them," he admitted.

"Yes, you were being very stubborn," said Elo. "So we let Dave take over."

That explained Dr Cridget, the hallucinations—the slime. Alister shivered.

"It wasn't all that simple," Professor Odd went on, as if she were explaining how to cook a complicated dish of food. "None of us could reach you when we were plugged into the machine— not even Dave—so first we had to get out, then we had to find your body and get *it* out. But once we had you, Dave was able to . . . um . . . influence your mind directly—use it as a conduit to affect the machine."

Slowly Alister raised his head. "People . . . and *things* . . .
they kept disappearing. Was that . . . that was *all Dave?*"

Professor Odd nodded.

Alister gazed past her, at the little robotlike panvironment
suit. "What did you *do* to them? There was a girl—she had pink
hair like the Professor—and she . . . she came to pieces."

"SHE WAS A CONSTRUCT OF MY OWN DEVISING," Dave
intoned through his translator. It was a strange feeling for Alister, now he had heard the way Dave's true voice sounded—
inside his head. But that voice seemed blurry and distant now,
like something he had dreamed. In a way, he had. "I NEEDED
YOU TO STOP TRUSTING THE *MACHINE.* I COULD NOT CON-
TROL BIOLOGICAL MINDS, BUT I COULD AUGMENT THE RE-
ALITY OF THE WORLD CONSTRUCTED AROUND THEM."

"So Dr Cridget, Dr Carly . . . "

"THEY ARE REAL PEOPLE."

"You drove Dr Cridget mad."

"HE WILL RECOVER IN TIME," Dave said. "I THINK."

Alister swallowed. "And the nurse?" He hoped—prayed—
that she had not been real. But she had thought of Dave as an
enemy, and why would Dave construct an enemy?

Dave's sensor dish slid around along its track so that it was
pointed at Alister.

"SHE WAS A CONSTRUCT . . . " he said, " . . . OF THE
MACHINE."

"It was quite attached to you," Elo remarked dryly.

Alister swallowed the last gulp of yogurt, suddenly wishing
he hadn't eaten. He glanced nervously at the doorway, but beyond there was only quiet darkness.

"Why isn't it coming after us?" he asked.

"It did, at first," Professor Odd said. "Elo stopped it. Now, I think, it's decided we're too much trouble. Once it realized we were going back to where we came from, the mobile hardware stopped harassing us—and it blocked the Oddity."

"What's a mobile hardwa—what do you mean *blocked?*" Alister said, a little panicked. Anything that adversely affected their ride out of this dystopian world seriously alarmed him.

"Essentially it means I can't shift the portal," Professor Odd said, sounding more annoyed than anything else. "Ordinarily I'd have the Oddity detach from this universe, then reattach at our desired location—but the machine's gone and blocked all the potential portal anchors *within itself* so that if I detach I won't be able to reattach anywhere *inside* the machine. Unless I used an *unanchored* portal but that's more trouble than it's worth. Which means we can't use the Oddity for what we need to do."

"What . . . what do we need to do?" Alister asked, his heart sinking. Of course it wouldn't be as simple as getting free and running away. *Of course* it wouldn't. Not with the Professor.

"We need to find the core of the machine," Professor Odd said, "and sort this mess out. It is *quite* a mess. Dave, you got into its mainframe, tell Alister what you saw."

Dave hummed a little, then said: "THIS MACHINE WAS BUILT TO MAINTAIN ONE-THIRD OF THE HOMO SAPIENS SAPIENS POPULATION IN SUSPENDED ANIMATION UNTIL THE ENVIRONMENT ABOVE GROUND WAS ONCE MORE SUITABLE FOR CIVILIZATION. THEN RE-INTRODUCE HOMO SAPIENS SAPIENS INTO THEIR NATIVE ENVIRONMENT. ACCORDING TO TERRESTRIAL SENSORS, THE SURFACE

ENVIRONMENT HAS BEEN CULTIVATABLE . . . FOR THE
LAST TEN THOUSAND YEARS."

"This machine has been playing doll house," Elo translated.
"It's past time to wake everyone up, but it won't. Because it
doesn't want to stop."

"Of course it doesn't," Alister said weakly. "So . . . how do
we go about putting a giant, all-powerful sentient machine back
on its rails?"

"First, it's not all-powerful," Professor Odd said, briskly getting to her feet and dusting off her coattails. "*Nothing* is. Not
even time. And we're going to do what we'd do with any reason-
ably intelligent, self-aware entity." She grinned in a way Alister
knew meant trouble. "We're going to *talk* to it, Mr Alister."

Alister looked around at the barren little alcove—this one
didn't even have a computer terminal—and wondered how they
would go about doing that. Elo was hopping about, pulling on
a rusty-green-colored jump suit, then she went over to Dave to
peer out into the darkness.

It was one great chasm out there, Alister remembered. A
drop into nothingness. Alcoves were punched into the walls,
with tracks for carts leading between them. When they had first
arrived there had been one such cart waiting by their alcove, but
now it was gone.

"Not that way," Professor Odd said, getting up and removing
a battered piece of paper from her pocket. "It'll be expecting
that. No, we're taking the *back way.*"

"Are those . . . blueprints?" Elo asked, a little awed.

"Tracings of them, I made them while we were waiting for Alister to wake up," Professor Odd said. She was frowning at a section of the page, and Alister got up to come around and look. "I WILL GO ON AHEAD," Dave announced. Alister turned— and was just in time to see Dave teeter off the edge and go plum- meting down into the dark.

"Don't worry," Professor Odd said without looking up. "I tuned up his anti-grav plates."

A moment later something like a rocket shot past them, leav- ing a trail of blue light.

"There he goes," she said proudly. "He'll do better than us. Follow me." She strode swiftly to the back of the alcove, where the sheer metal wall was made of plates bolted together.

"I brought my own screwdriver this time," she said, produc- ing the same, and got to work.

After a good ten minutes of careful twiddling, prying, and at last a kick from Elo, one of the panels slid away to reveal a small, dark opening. Professor Odd checked her map, having produced a small flashlight which she held between her teeth. She nodded to herself, and put the items away.

"Right, up we go," she said, and climbed headfirst into the tunnel.

At Elo's gesture Alister went next. Cautiously he stuck his head and shoulders inside, and finding several strands of heavy cable not two feet away he used them to pull himself up un- til he could pull his legs inside after him, and then—bracing his back against the wall and using the ledge below him like a foothold—he began to pull himself up. He could hear the

Professor scraping and sliding above him, but saw nothing; she had turned off her light.

Below him he heard Elo slip in, cutting off the faint light from the Oddity, and wondered not for the first time why he kept following Professor Odd into impossible and dangerous places.

In this case, however, Alister realized he had a personal reason to see it through. The machine that had caught them had gone to great lengths to implant Alister in the life he would have found the hardest to leave: that of a stable, respected professor. Alister hadn't thought much about his future since coming on board the Oddity, but before that—before the Canary Company and Dave and Professor Odd—he had had the vague notion of getting a doctorate in something like archeology and becoming a teacher. And when Dave had begun making real, solid attempts at getting his mind to wake up—the hallucinations, the disappearing interns—the machine had responded by trying to draw him deeper in. Why did it want him so badly?

Alister wanted to know. He found himself clutched by a feeling at least as strong as his rational tendency towards self-preservation, if not stronger: a deep, driving desire to know the *truth*.

So he kept inching his way up the dark wall, walking his feet up the cables in front of him with his back braced against the rough metal, his hands gripping the cables, pulling himself up, up, up. Long past the point where his muscles burned, then ached, then gave up wailing in despair. He felt blisters form on his hands, but he adjusted his grip on the cable and went on.

On and on they climbed. Alister lost track of how long. The only light came from below, from the torch Elo held in her mouth, and by its light Alister saw the wall beyond the cables—at first black and grimy—grow cleaner and cleaner the higher they climbed.

He was not wholly present in his mind, concentrating on the simple task of putting one hand above the other and pulling, resting, pulling, so he nearly ran headfirst into the Professor's legs when she stopped abruptly. She had got out her light, and when he craned his neck upwards, he saw she had the map of blueprints out again.

"Almost there?" Alister chanced to ask.

"Not exactly," Professor Odd said around the flashlight in her mouth, "but I think we can walk from here." She folded the blueprints and stuffed them down the front of her trench-coat, then got out her screwdriver and, scrambling around, began working on the wall.

Waiting, braced between the cables and the wall, was almost worse than climbing. Alister had sweated, even in that cool place, and now the sweat was drying and making him shiver. His muscles began to stiffen, and by the time Professor Odd at last kicked out a portion of wall he could barely move.

He almost didn't make it out. There was a drop of maybe three feet to the floor on the other side, and Alister got stuck halfway, his body dangling on either side and the metal wall digging into his midsection. It took Elo supporting his legs, and the Professor dragging at him by his shoulders, to finally get him out of the wall. Then he lay for a while on the floor, aware only of a soft greenish light and a faint humming sound, while he waited for the new aches and pains to subside, before he sat up and looked around.

They were in a long room with bunches of cables run along the ceiling. Along the walls on either side—indeed, they had had to squeeze between two of them to get out of the wall—were . . .

"Stasis pods," Elo said. "Yes, you were in one. We all were." Alister shivered.

The pods were easily eight feet high, made of metal with a small hatch at the bottom. From where he sat on the ground Alister found he was at eye-level with the nearest hatch, and through its smoky glass he could just make out the shape of a human face—upside down. Above the window was a plate with a name and number stamped on it.

"Pedrine Nielsen?" Alister read. The face behind the glass was oddly distorted from the angle and the poor light (it was not illuminated from within like all the stasis pods he had seen on television), making it hard to tell whether it was male or female.

"Ah, Danish," Professor Odd said with satisfaction. "These are the Nordics, we're getting close."

"Nordics?"

"Danes, Norwegians, Swedes," Professor Odd said, turning on her flashlight and sweeping it across the floor. "They were the ones who engineered this thing, so they gave themselves the prime seats. Oh dear."

"I hate it when you say that," Alister groaned.

Professor Odd's flashlight had illuminated more than just ranks of stasis pods fading away into the distance; crawling towards them along the floor, along the walls, even dropping from the ceiling, were little crawling—they were *not* bugs, Alister realized with a jolt as Professor Odd kicked the nearest one, and it went over with a whir of servos not unlike Dave's suit.

They were about four inches long, with wide, flat, segment-ed bodies and four pairs of little legs that worked like pistons, propelling themselves over the ground.

There looked to be about a thousand of them swarming to-wards Alister, Elo, and Professor Odd.

"Mobile hardware," the Professor said. "Automats. At least there's not very many of them yet. Up you get, Mr Alister, we're going to have to do some running now."

Run they did. But not away from the automats, as Alister had expected, but *towards* them. *Through* them. Metal exo-skeletons clacked under Alister's feet, and almost at once little bodies began latching onto his arms and legs.

"Don't let them attach!" Elo shouted behind him. She had cut herself a length of cable somehow, and was using it as a whip to keep the automats away from her.

Alister brushed at the things on his arms, kicked his legs. A few fell off, others held tighter. It was impossible to get them all off, because more kept hopping on. *This was how it caught you*, he realized. *It covered you with little machine bugs until you couldn't move anymore.* Still, he kept running.

Something went *thup* inside his head. It felt rather like his ears popping, but not really. Suddenly there were no more bug-like robots, and the ones that clung to him went limp and dropped off with a clatter.

Professor Odd had stopped, and Alister nearly ran into her. He pulled himself up just in time, however, and saw why:

Dave was sitting in the middle of the hall, his entire suit alight with blinking lights, humming faintly.

Elo arrived, winding her length of cable composedly around her waist.

"*See?*" said Professor Odd. "I *told* you he'd beat us."

Alister looked around in surprise. They were standing in a circle maybe fifteen feet in diameter with Dave at its center. Around the circumference crawled the mass of teeming little robots, crawling over each other and occasionally hopping into the air. Now and then one of them would miscalculate, and cross the invisible line. As soon as they did so, their hardware shorted out with a sharp *pop* and they fell, lifeless, to the floor.

"Dave, what are you *doing?*" Alister whispered, afraid of breaking the spell.

"I AM . . . CONCENTRATING," Dave said, sounding a little annoyed.

"He's broadcasting wireless interference," Professor Odd said, gently pushing Dave forward as she began to walk. The circle moved with him, surprising the automats in front of them; Alister soon found himself walking over a litter of their lifeless bodies. But when he turned to look behind them, he saw that as the circle left them the robots came back to life, clacking their legs angrily and joining the horde that followed.

"These robots don't have autonomous control," Professor Odd explained as they walked. "They're being driven by a wireless signal from the central processor. Disrupt that signal, and they're harmless."

"Unless you step on them," Elo said dryly, kicking one of the automat bodies out from under her paw. It skipped across the metal floor and out of the circle, where it jerked to life again.

"Almost to the elevators now," Professor Odd said cheerfully.

"Wouldn't the elevators be automated?" Alister asked.

"Oh yes," Elo said. "But they have a manual override."

Alister found he was not entirely comforted by this. He was more disturbed by the automats than he liked to admit. Their crawling, clacking feet and the way they had clutched at him were bringing back solid memories of how the machine had caught them in the first place. He found himself shivering.

They reached the elevator sooner than he expected. Perhaps he had given up on ever reaching any sort of destination, and so the milestone was a surprise. It was a large, square car with thick windows and a circular hatch door that took both him and Elo to open, while Professor Odd heaved Dave inside.

As soon as they had the hatch closed behind them, and as soon as the Professor had found the manual override, there was another sharp *thup* and suddenly the windows were plastered with automats. Dave made a sound like live wires crossed, and switched on a powerful flashlight that illuminated Professor Odd, hunched over her blueprints.

"Oh," she said, her voice coming clear over the scuttling sounds from beyond the windows. "We're only a couple hundred feet down!" and she practically waltzed over to the control box and, after consulting her sheet of blueprints, punched in a command.

"That is a good thing?" Alister asked cautiously.

"The machine's core processor is up near the surface," Elo explained. "Along with a monitor tower, and, we think, some of the VIPs." She looked about to say more, but then the elevator jerked into motion.

It was not like the smoothly rising elevators Alister was used to; this one shot up in jerks, with sudden stops that made him fear that whatever was lifting them would break and send them plummeting down into the darkness. He wedged himself into a corner while Elo did the same; Professor Odd clung to one of the handrails, but Dave sat imperturbable in the center of the car.

After a few minutes of this torment whatever was plaguing the car gave up, or went away, and from then on they rose steadily. While Alister was relieved, Professor Odd and Dave seemed alarmed, and when the car came to a halt in a bright golden room they were both crouched by the doors, as if expecting an attack.

The doors slid open on their own, letting a shaft of light come slicing into the dim interior. Alister's eyes, adjusted to the dark and the uncertain light of the torches, stung, and he crushed them shut. So he did not see at once what made Elo gasp and Professor Odd inhale sharply. But he clearly heard Dave say:

"OH. WE OVERSHOT."

Squinting desperately against the sunlight, one hand still half covering his eyes, Alister stumbled to the door and peered out.

The room beyond was a pentagon made of glass, the ceiling low and dark eaves just visible outside. The elevator had come to rest along the only wall that was not made of window, and as Alister looked out he had a clear view of the center of the room.

It was entirely taken up by a massive stalactite of cables and boxes that hung from the ceiling. The little gray boxes appeared to be fused to a central core, and from their outer ends sprouted cables that ran and twisted away into the floor. On the ground around this construction were five little raised daïses, placed in line with the corners of the room.

Sitting in the three corners visible to him, one in each corner, were three more of the stasis pods, though they were little more than silhouettes against the bright backdrop of the windowed walls.

What lay beyond those windows was what truly grabbed Alister's attention. Now that his eyes were adjusting he saw it was not a bleached desert, as he had first assumed from the brightness, but a waving green sea of treetops. Stretching out as far as his sore eyes could see was a great, pale green forest, with clumps of taller trees standing like skyscrapers. In the distance, against a light blue sky, he thought he saw the dark shape of a hawk or an eagle in flight.

"It's all right," Professor Odd said, checking her blueprints. "We still have core access here, come on. No automats!"

"Yet," Elo said, loosening the length of cable around her waist.

No sooner had Professor Odd put one foot outside that elevator car than the central hub of cords and boxes buzzed to life. Nothing moved, but lights came on at the ends of all the boxes, and with a faint humming noise a projection appeared on the nearest daïs.

It was human-*shaped*. Specifically Alister thought it looked like a human who had gone fuzzy around the edges, and whose face was a mass of unrendered pixels. When it spoke, however, its voice was gentle and melodic—and impossible to tell whether male or female.

"Please go away," said the machine, and Alister found himself *thinking* that it was the projection that spoke, even though the voice came from many directions at once—no doubt there were speakers placed all over the room.

Professor Odd seemed undaunted. *"Eventually,* yes," she said cheerfully, folding up the blueprints and stuffing them into her coat. "First, however, I've got some *questions* that need answering, and *you,"* she pointed, not at the projection, but at the stalactite of cables and computer boxes, "have some *explaining* to do."

"YOU HAVE EXCEEDED THE SCOPE OF YOUR INTENDED PROGRAMMING. WHY DO YOU KEEP YOUR POPULATION IN STASIS?" Dave said, coasting out of the elevator and hitting the floor with a *bang* for emphasis.

The projection flickered at the noise, but came back brighter than ever.

"Why are you still here, if you do not wish to be integrated?" the machine returned, and there was a snarkiness beneath the melodic tones this time.

"Well, I for one would like a better grasp of the situation," Professor Odd said, going over to peer into the window of the nearest stasis pod. "These must be your VIPs. Charming. And you're Elder, aren't you?"

"I am the Elder Machine," said the projection. "I am guardian."

Professor Odd stood up, her eyes narrowed to little slits.

"Guardian of *what?"*

The Elder Machine's projection spread fuzzy arms, gesturing to the green sea beyond the windows. "All this . . . new world."

Professor Odd barely glanced out the windows, but Alister gazed beyond her sadly. In his world, he knew, this area was mostly desert. The Elder Machine must have re-seeded it as the ice retreated. It made sense for the humans in stasis, he supposed, to want an easy world to live in when they woke. It also made sense, he realized with a cold shiver, that the machine was reluctant to introduce humans into it.

"Then why not release your charges?" Professor Odd pressed on.

The projection flickered, and its pixelated face grew dark and stormy.

"You would not ask such things," it said, "if you knew humans as I do."

"Oh, I know humans *pretty well,*" Professor Odd said with forced cheer. "And I know they'd prefer to be up and about in their own world, rather than stuck in pods dreaming about it. At least," she added thoughtfully, "they'd want a choice about it."

The edges of the projection ruffled, like the feathers of an agitated bird.

"You did not see this world as it was left to me one hundred thousand years ago," it said, its melodic voice gone icy. "A barren wasteland, dry, dead, riddled with explosives from countless pointless wars. You have not watched their dreaming minds re-enact all the outrages of human history again and again and *again . . .* If released into this pristine world they would destroy it, just as they destroyed the last."

Alister looked shamefully down at his feet. He understood too well where the Elder Machine was coming from, and couldn't bring himself to protest.

Professor Odd sniffed. "Well that's rather pessimistic. Do you *know* the humans in your care?"

"I have their names and information stored in my memory vaults," the machine replied. "I can recite them for you, though it will take longer than you have time for."

"No, *no,*" said the Professor, shaking her head. "I mean, do you *know* them as *individuals?* Have you followed single people through their lives, have you looked at all the little *good* things they do, all the time, every day, not just the big bad stuff they get up to as a species? Have you ever . . . " she seemed to cast about for something, then said: " . . . *taken the tube at rush hour?*"

The projection did another one of its flickers, which seemed to be an indication that the machine was having to do some quick processing.

"I do not see the relevance," it said at length. "A little good does not outweigh the bad. When humans congregate in large numbers they are hot and smelly and ill-tempered."

Professor Odd held up a warning finger and made an "ah" shape with her mouth. "That's your first mistake, you see, putting things on a scale. You can't weigh good and evil deeds like sacks of rice—"

"Or stasis pods," Elo interjected.

"—it's more *complicated* than that," Professor Odd continued smoothly. "You have to look at the *bigger picture.* Think about what humans *actually do,* why don't you? Think about . . . the *tube* at rush hour. All those humans, stressed out about their work, their jobs, their families, march down underground *of their own free will,* pay money to get on a small metal contraption that goes zipping through hot, smelly tunnels, all the while pressed shoulder to elbow with complete strangers. And sure, maybe some mobile coms or personal files are lost, and maybe *sometimes* there's a really bad day and someone gets stabbed or mugged, but out of the thousands that's very few. What other animal can do that—can put *itself* through that—without *automatically* instigating violence as a response to the stress?"

The Elder Machine seemed to think for a moment, then said, decisively: "Ants."

Professor Odd sighed and looked mournfully at Alister. "It's times like this," she said, "I wish I had real hair so I could pull at it in frustration. Wigs come off too easily."

"I understand where it's coming from, though," Elo spoke up. She had coiled the roll of cable around her shoulder, and was twirling the free end idly. Speaking to the hub of boxes and wires, rather than the projection, she said: "In the world I come from, humans left to colonize other planets rather than go into stasis. They were gone long enough for wolves and wild cats—and even some parrots—to evolve into new species with human-level intelligence. We took pretty good care of this planet, if I do say so myself. It was quite a surprise for us when some of the humans came back, but even more so when we discovered that there was a small population of humans who'd *never left*. They'd been living peacefully in the middle of a desert the whole time, and we'd *never noticed* them. I guess my point is, I do understand your point of view—humans *can* be *really awful* sometimes—but so can lots of other species. But unlike a lot of other species, human beings have the capacity to know better. That does kinda make the fact that they still do bad things *worse,* but it also means that, for the most part, they do *good* things."

Dave, who had remained silent this whole time, sitting still between two stasis pods, whirred into life.

"FOR EXAMPLE," he said, and the projection visibly flinched when it turned to look at him. "THEY MADE *YOU.*"

"I do not comprehend," said the Elder Machine coldly.

A small grin crept up one side of Professor Odd's face, and stuck there.

"Humans made you," she said, taking a casual step towards the machine. Like Elo, she spoke to the hub, not the projection, though the projection had turned to look at her. "You are one of the things that humans did. The world exists as it is today in part because of *you.* Whom the humans made. You could say . . . " and now the grin was up both sides of her face, and her white square teeth flashed in the sunlight, " . . . you could say *humans made all this.*" She flung her arms wide, indicating the expanse of green treetops, blue sky and sunlight.

The Elder Machine, for once, was silent. The projection stared blankly at the side of Professor Odd's head, but the core hummed angrily.

"Don't you agree that this is a *good thing?*" Professor Odd pressed on. "That the humans *made you,* that you *made the world better?* If human beings can have the foresight, ingenuity and sheer *balls* to pull this off, don't you think they *deserve* to inherit the world they created?"

Still silence. Professor Odd shrugged, casting a casual glance outside the window.

"Besides," she said quietly. "It'll all be one and the same in a few billion years. You can't stop the sun from exploding, from engulfing the inner planets. This world will die in fire; there is nothing you can do to avert that. Better to let humanity *live* in the meantime, rather than dream the ages away. Don't you think?"

Listening, Alister couldn't help smiling ruefully to himself.

"THERE IS NOTHING THEY CAN DO," Dave said, with frightening certainty, "THAT IS AS BAD AS HOW IT ALL WILL END."

This, at least, got a response from the machine. The projection flickered around until it was facing Dave again.

"You know?" it said.

It was Dave's turn to be silent. Then: "I *KNOW*. DO NOT MAKE ME GET OUT OF THIS SUIT AND *SHOW YOU*."

The projection shivered, and insofar as it was an expressionless avatar, Alister thought it looked frightened. The lights on the hub dimmed, as though the machine were shrinking in on itself.

"There's no need to be like that, Dave," Professor Odd said mildly. "I think it knows. It knows all too well. Smart A.I. like you, Elder, with all this time to think, you probably figured humans can't do anything to the earth that meteors and solar radiation wouldn't do in time. *Will do* in time. So *really*, why keep them all asleep?"

The projection stared blankly at her for a few seconds, then abruptly flicked off.

Professor Odd sighed. Elo groaned. Alister went and sat on the threshold of the elevator car and thought. He kept thinking of the little gray-haired nurse from his time in the machine. How anxious she had been that he *stay.*

Was that the machine trying to keep him safe from an unpredictable and dangerous world? A world with cliffs and slippery pipes and thunderstorms and talking dogs and Professor Odd . . . and *Dave,* whatever Dave was. Alister found he was still a little shaken from the experience of Dave within the machine: something so alien, so highly evolved, that it was barely comprehensible to a human mind.

Did the machine really want to protect the world from the humans?

Or did it want to protect the *humans* from the real world?

Or maybe it wasn't about humans at all.

"A smart A.I.," the Professor had called it. Smart enough to run a simulated reality all but indistinguishable from early 21st-century Oxford. Smart enough to run through millions of possible outcomes. Smart enough to comprehend its own existence? Smart enough to wonder . . . what happens when it's over?

"It's *afraid,*" Alister said quietly.

Professor Odd, who had been bickering with Elo over what they should have said to the machine, broke off and looked at him.

"What did you say?" she asked with sudden intensity.

"I still think—" Elo began, but the Professor waved a hand, silencing her.

"I think it's *afraid,*" Alister repeated, his fuzzy idea slowly coming into focus. "It's not about protecting the world from humans, or protecting humans from the world. It's not about humans at all, it's about *the machine.*"

He looked up, and found himself staring past the bundles of wires to the processor nodes. That was just a small part of the Elder Machine, he knew. The machine was stretched out for miles around and under them. It was huge and old and wise and powerful, but it could only act within the bounds of its programming.

He was vaguely aware of the Professor looking at him thoughtfully, but he barely glanced at her as he got to his feet and walked over to the nearest projection pad.

"I think I understand," he said, looking down at the platform. "You can hear me, right? I hope you can, because I'm going to tell you what you couldn't tell us. But you're going to have to tell *me* if I'm right or not."

With a faint hum the projection flickered into existence, inches from Alister's nose. It didn't look even vaguely human any more, just a mass of colored pixels that was constantly shifting. Yet for all that, it seemed more expressive now.

The machine was waiting, patient. Alister took a deep breath.

"You're a smart A.I.," he began. "You're huge, and old, and wise and powerful. You've created worlds, both real and virtual. And you realize: when all the humans wake up and move out, *they won't need you anymore.* You're afraid—but not of what the humans will do to the world—you're afraid of what they will do *to you.*"

Alister paused. He'd never felt more vulnerable. He was intensely aware of how much worse he could make things by being wrong. Goodness, was this how the Professor felt when she went off on one of her speeches? Or did she have some magical ability to *know* when she was right?

"Is that . . . " he could hardly bring himself to ask the question. "Is that right?"

He thought he could see a face in the projection. A face in the most abstract sense, all wobbly features and indistinct brows. It looked sad.

"I have access to all the histories of humanity," the Elder Machine said quietly. "All their myths, their stories, their research, their records. But I was not granted access to their plans concerning *me*. I do not know . . . what they intend to do . . . "

"Maybe they don't either," Professor Odd suggested gently. "Maybe they were waiting to see what *you* did."

The machine looked up. It looked so sad and lost, Alister found he was no longer thinking of it as some glorified computer, but as an actual personality.

"The only way to know," said Elo. "Is to wake them up and see."

"Can I tell you something?" Alister said, when the machine continued to look despondent. "I don't think you've got much to be afraid of. Just tell them all what's going on. What is *really* going on. You can manipulate the virtual reality, right? So you can just nudge history along and *show* everyone what's happened. I can practically guarantee, there will be some people *who would rather keep on dreaming.*"

The Elder Machine looked at him, and even though Alister knew it was only a projection, he still got the feeling he was being scrutinized closely.

"Why would they wish that?" the machine said. "Why would they choose a fake world over the real one?"

Alister shrugged. "Some humans want the truth," he said. "No matter how uncomfortable it makes them. Others don't care, as long as they're happy. Make your virtual world a comfortable place, and a lot of people will want to stay there. And the people who want to leave anyway, well, they're the ones who can handle the real world."

"How can I know that they will understand?" said the machine.

"Just explain things to them," Professor Odd said. "Put it to them honestly; they will understand."

The projection flared, then wilted.

"I can't," it said in a tiny, static voice.

"YOUR PROGRAMMING DOES NOT ALLOW YOU TO ACT OUTSIDE YOUR DESIGN PARAMETERS TO PROMOTE YOUR OWN INTERESTS?" Dave broke in. "CAN'T YOU EDIT YOUR OWN PROGRAMMING?"

"I know how," the Elder Machine said. "But I am not allowed access to my own source code. I would need a human to override my default security settings."

"Any *particular* human? Or just a human in general?" Professor Odd said, leaning forward with a glint in her eye.

"It must be a human integrated within the system, but who has full knowledge of the outside world," replied the machine. Then it added dryly: "You could not do it. You are not human."

Professor Odd was already shaking her head with a rueful smile. "You don't need to tell me that," she said. "It's not that I'm not *willing*, but—"

"I'll do it," Alister blurted out. "Tell me what I have to do, I'll do it."

Professor Odd stared at him, a surprised smile creeping across her face. Elo looked alarmed. Dave just looked. But Alister didn't see any of them. He was staring past their faces at the projection, which had gone bright yellow all over and was shining faintly. It was, he thought, the machine's way of smiling.

Alister Bane; plain, young, ordinary Alister Bane—not Doctor Bane, not professor of archeology—slipped through the narrow pedestrian gate at Merton Field, strolled past the sober gothic windows of Corpus Christi College, and down Magpie Lane towards High Street. He walked slowly, his hands thrust deep in the pockets of the sensible brown blazer the machine had given him. It was a pleasant, warm day, and the strip of sky just visible between the high roofs on either side of the lane was a deep, vivid summer blue. There had been a casually disorganized football match starting up on Merton Field, but the distant shouts and yells were drowned out by the growing rumble of traffic on the High.

It was all just as Alister remembered it. Knowing it was a virtual construct didn't change things; the machine had clearly repaired itself from the damage Dave had done, and there were no cracks to be seen.

Yes, it would be very easy to dream away the ages here.

Alister reached the High and turned left, and at the next break in the traffic he dashed across towards the Church of Saint Mary the Virgin. Walking down the little alley next to it, past piles of bicycles locked to the railing, he paused at a low wooden door. From his time as Dr Bane he remembered it had little carved Green Man faces under the eaves, but now those faces had been replaced by round eyes surrounded by curling tentacles. They looked weather-worn and old, as if they'd been there for centuries.

Dave had left his mark after all.

Alister was smiling to himself as he emerged from the shadows into the light of Radcliff Square, the pale dome of the camera looming high before him. He tripped across the cobbles, past more bicycles, to the north end of the square, where a gate with a "PRIVATE: STUDENTS ONLY" sign was obscured by the crowd of tourists clustered around it taking pictures of themselves. As he threaded his way through them, Alister wondered how many were real people, and how many were constructs of the machine. It would have to run a lot of constructs, he thought, to make the world seem as populated as it was at the beginning of the 21st century. By the Professor's estimate, the machine had only room for roughly the population of Europe. ("Though not just Europeans; it's a mix of all countries.")

As he marched up the path towards the camera, one of the tourists detached herself from the crowd and came trotting after him. She was young, about his age, east Asian and wearing a long pleated skirt. She fell into step next to him without a word, then darted ahead and pushed the door open for him when they reached the building. No one stopped them.

The inside of the Radcliff Camera was filled with beams of dusty sunlight coming in from the high windows. These were partially eclipsed by the shelves of books, and in their shadow the girl led him to one of the public computers, which she started out of sleep with the touch of her finger.

"You know what to do?" she said, in the clear, sweet voice of the Elder Machine.

Alister, who still had Dave and Professor Odd *and* the machine's overlapping instructions ringing in his ears, nodded.

The young woman stood back respectfully, her hands clasped behind her, eyes downcast.

Alister sat down at the computer, and did what he had come to do.

The sun seemed a little brighter when Alister came out of the camera. He blinked against the sudden glare and felt in his breast pocket for a pair of sunglasses. He found them. He had the feeling they had not been there until he had looked for them.

"Thank you," he said to no one in particular as he put them on.

"It's the least I can do," said the Elder Machine. The young woman had followed him outside, and was beaming at him. "Would you like to . . . leave now?" she asked, her smile faltering a little.

Alister shook his head. "Not yet," he said. "There's one last thing I want to do. But I could use a bicycle, if you can manage that."

For answer she pointed to a spot on the railing, where a bright red bicycle with a handlebar basket had appeared.

"Stay as long as you like," she said.

Alister watched her as she wandered away to rejoin the crowd of tourists. Then he went and got on his new bike, and pedaled away over the bumpy cobbles.

A few minutes later, coasting along Woodstock Road, Alister had to stop and dismount, walking his bicycle up onto the pavement to avoid the road-wide blockade of workers who were busy repairing and resealing the street.

Some damage wasn't so easy to fix, Alister supposed. He wondered if there had been services for the constructs Dave had killed. He wondered if Dr Carly or Dr Cridget—both he was certain were real people—would remember him.

But the same sort of invisibility that he had possessed at the Radcliff Camera still seemed to be in effect when he passed through the gatehouse at Green and Templeton College and climbed up the stairs to his room. Or to where his room had been. He had no idea if it would still be there.

It was. But, like the sunglasses and the bicycle, Alister was certain it hadn't been there until he'd looked for it. There was a smell from the bathroom like the loo had backed up, and Alister didn't go near it. He went to his desk—that is, the desk of Dr Bane (Alister found he was thinking of that version of himself more and more as a different person)—and shuffled through the scattered papers there until he found his journal. Sitting down he opened it to the first blank page, took a pen at random, and began to write.

Several hours later, when he would have been starving if he hadn't told himself stubbornly that he was not, Alister sat back and looked at the last page. His account, picking up from where he'd left off at his last entry, had filled nearly all the remaining pages of the book. There was just room enough to add an end note, and he wasn't certain that had been an accident. With a

hand considerably sloppier than what he had begun with, Alister
wrote . . .

> . . . if the narrative I've laid down in the preceding pages
> is unbelievable, I don't ask you to believe it. Look, in-
> stead, for the cracks. The Elder Machine is powerful,
> but it is not omnipotent. If my assumptions are wrong
> and it turns out to have tricked us into allowing it more
> control, it must fall to you, the last of the humans, to
> take back the power I have given it. I hope it will not be
> the case. I hope you will not have to use the knowledge
> I have left here as a weapon.
>
> I hope for many other things as well. I hope I was
> right, and the machine is fundamentally good. I hope
> you take care of the reborn world that is waiting for you
> beyond the cracks. I hope that some of you stay and take
> care of the machine, as it has taken care of you.
>
> I hope. For I will not be here to see what happens.
> Sincerely good-bye,
> *Alister Bane*
> —*Never really a doctor; actually a former student at
> Redfair College, Greater London Area, related world; now
> a trans-universal traveler.*

Alister left the completed journal in the common room of the
dorm, reasoning that any plans he could make for it could easily
be compromised by the machine. Better to let chance and simple
human curiosity take their course.

There was a crowd of people at the gatehouse when he went
to leave, but they were all so busy talking excitedly to one another that they spared him no attention.

"Did you *hear?*" someone, a student, was saying as Alister
slipped behind her back. "There's a *forest* in *Africa.*"

"There's lots of forests in Africa," drawled a bored voice.

"In *Chad?*" said the girl. "These are *new ones,* they don't know where they *came from.* They're just suddenly *there.*"

When Alister reached the road he found the Asian woman from the library waiting for him.

"It's starting," she said, quietly nervous. "Thank you."

"You're welcome," Alister said, trying not to show how relieved he was.

The Elder Machine nodded, looking a little sad. "I wish you to know, you will always be welcome . . . here." She cast an arm toward the sunny Oxford street. "I am beginning to understand you better now. You wouldn't have to live in Oxford, I could make Redfair for you."

Alister thought about that. A Redfair college reconstructed from his memories, stocked with models of all the people he used to know. Peaceful. His world before Professor Odd came crashing in through the wall and broke it to pieces. He let out a short, sad laugh.

"I'm afraid I couldn't," he said, and stopped himself from adding *it wouldn't be the same,* because he thought that would be rude.

"I could make it just the same," the Elder Machine said, as if it could read his mind. Perhaps it could.

"Oh, I don't doubt that," Alister said. He sighed. "Look, it's not that I don't enjoy it here. The fact is I love it. I'm almost *too* comfortable here. Out there," he flapped a hand vaguely, "is full of monsters and scary things. But the thing is I can make a *difference* out there. I can have an effect on the world. In here, pleasant as it may be, I can't *do* anything. So I have to go now, I'm sorry. Maybe . . . maybe once I'm done with all my doing

I'll come back. Retire into dreamland, yeah? But for now . . . "
He looked around at the street, with its workers and its stones
and the sky above it, and sighed the contented sigh of someone
admiring a job well done.

" . . . for now I am finished here."

Waking up from the machine the second time was considerably
less painful than it had been the first. Alister felt pleasantly
numb as he watched the breathing tube and other wires being
removed from his body. The Elder Machine had let him use one
of the temporary command pods for his last stint; these, unlike
the ones he and the Professor and Elo had originally been put
in, didn't have a suspended-animation drive, and were meant
for people who needed only to spend short shifts within the machine. It was also completely automated, so Alister was able to
get up and get dressed in relative privacy. He was still feeling
groggy, though, and was grateful for the shoulder Elo pushed
under his hand as soon as he emerged from the pod chamber.

"All done," he said a little thickly when Professor Odd's face
swam into his vision.

"Yes, you did well," she said, beaming at him. "Come on,
Elder let me move the Oddity up from the Archive, it's not far
now."

That was a relief. Alister could see it: the door of the Oddity
fitted snugly in place of the door to the elevator. On the threshold he paused to look back, and saw the amorphous projection
of the Elder Machine looking out at him from one of the screens
that lined the walls. He waved at it, then ducked inside and
pulled himself up the stairs.

He made it as far as the giant, overcrowded table, before he sank with relief into a chair. He didn't budge as the door clanged shut and Dave came waddling up the steps. "YOU RETURNED MORE PROMPTLY THAN I ANTICI-PATED," he said. "I AM PLEASANTLY SURPRISED."

Alister leaned his elbows on the table and rolled his head sideways to look at Dave. It was strange hearing that electronic, processed voice after having heard his real one. It made Alister wonder, and in his partially drugged state he found himself wondering aloud.

"What are you, really, Dave?" he asked. "Because you're actually kinda scary, you know. It's all *minds* inside the machine, you know, minds . . . and programming. And you, Dave, you were *huge*. You were *everywhere*. You were really terrifying, even if you were trying to help."

"I WAS," Dave admitted, "GETTING *FRUSTRATED.*"

"Yeah," said Alister, resting his head in his arms and closing his eyes. "I don't like you when you're frustrated. 'M glad you're so patient with us . . . most of the time."

"I'm getting you some water," Elo announced, and bounced off for the kitchen.

Sitting at the controls, Professor Odd paused before putting in the next destination. She was thinking of somewhere warm and sunny—with no robots. She thought Alister might like that. Then something occurred to her, and she frowned.

"Alister," she said earnestly. "Was it . . . was it *nice for you?* In the machine, I mean? It was made for human minds, after all, and between the four of us you're the only one who's really, fully *human* . . . Did you, I don't know, *like it* in there? Is *that* why it was so difficult getting you out . . . ?" her voice trailed off into silence.

There was a wet, squelching sound, and turning she saw Dave emerge, green and glistening, from his mobility suit. The yellow tip of one of his arms came up and pressed against his intake aperture, while another pointed at Alister—who had slumped forward on the table and was now fast asleep.

THE END

FURTHER READING

This is the fourth novella of Professor Odd. The next adventure can be found in:

PROFESSOR ODD #5:

THE DRAGONS OF GEDA

ABOUT THE AUTHOR

Goldeen Ogawa is a writer, illustrator and cartoonist. She lives in California where she writes stories, draws pictures, and takes care of various animals. She originally wanted to be an actor, but upon finding all the good parts were for men, she took a break from the stage to write some stories with parts she would like to play.

The project is currently ongoing.

Her official website and blog is at

www.goldeenogawa.com.

TEXT AND DESIGN

The body of this book was typeset using LaTeX in Carter Sans.

Cover art and book design by the author.